www.randomhouse.com/kids

Library of Congress Cataloging-in-Publication Data

Lionni, Leo, 1910–1999

Frederick and his friends : four favorite fables / Leo Lionni ; with an introduction by Eric Carle.

p.   cm.

One sound disc (digital ; 4 3/4 in.) of word-for-word stories in front cover pocket.

Set of four titles previously published independently, three of which were "Caldecott honor book" winners.

Contents: Frederick—Swimmy—Fish is fish—Alexander and the wind-up mouse.

ISBN 0-375-82299-2

1. Children's stories, American. [1. Animals—Fiction. 2. Short stories.] I. Title.

PZ7.L6634 Fp 2002

[E]—dc21   2002022337

Manufactured in the United States of America

October 2002

10   9   8   7   6   5   4   3   2

First Edition

FREDERICK and His Friends

Four Favorite Fables by Leo Lionni

WITH A NOTE OF APPRECIATION BY ERIC CARLE

Alfred A. Knopf ⤳ New York

CONTENTS

Note of Appreciation by Eric Carle

Frederick

Swimmy

Fish Is Fish

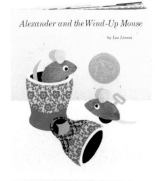

Alexander and the Wind-Up Mouse

In Appreciation of Leo Lionni

Leo Lionni (the name alone is sheer poetry!) saw himself as someone who was "between worlds." Born to a gentile mother and a Jewish father in Amsterdam in 1910, Leo grew up speaking Dutch. A year with his grandmother in Brussels taught him French. Moving on to Philadelphia, he learned English. Then, back in Europe, he lived in Italy and studied in Switzerland, where he learned Italian and German, and earned his college degree in economics but dreamed of art and of being an artist.

In 1939, fate brought Lionni back to the United States with his young wife and their two small children, where he became art director for *Fortune* magazine after World War II. Commuting back and forth between an apartment in New York City and a farmhouse in Tuscany, he was torn between his fascination with the world of commercial art and his love for the world of fine arts, of creating his own painting and sculpture.

Then one day, on the spur of the moment, while on a train from Grand Central Station to Greenwich, Connecticut, Leo Lionni invented *Little Blue and Little Yellow* to entertain his two small and restless grandchildren, Annie and Pippo. With that book, which was published in 1959, and with each book that followed, Lionni discovered his center and his soul, touching the source of all creativity: one's childhood. He not only resolved the dilemma of his creative life between worlds but also established himself securely as a member of the twentieth-century art community.

Whether drawn, painted, or illustrated in collage, each of his books is self-consistent, a world unto itself. Leo Lionni is a master of many techniques. With each book he breaks the mold of the traditional picture book. The graphic designer, painter, sculptor, world traveler, lecturer, raconteur par excellence, and magician unleashes his creative force in wise original fables and serenely crafted pictures. By adding a dash of exquisite yet simple and clear typography, he transforms each page into a drama of singular beauty, with the audience holding its breath as scene after scene unfolds across the stage. And when the curtain descends, the audience responds in joyous applause. And so will you, you who hold in your hands this very book containing four of Lionni's finest picture books.

Here is *Swimmy:* a tiny, insignificant fish in the vast and wide ocean who is ingenious enough to fend off the big, bad bully. *Alexander and the Wind-Up Mouse* is a new twist on Aesop's "The City Mouse and the Country Mouse" in which two mice form an unlikely friendship; Lionni adds a bit of sorcery and—voilà! *Fish Is Fish* confirms how futile it is to view the world only from one's own point of view; this is all acted out by hilarious, clown-like creatures. In *Frederick*, a mouse who is a poet from the tip of his nose to the end of his tail demonstrates that a seemingly purposeless life is indeed far from that—and that we live not by bread alone!

Fifty years ago, when as a young man I arrived in New York City from Germany, I saw and admired the brilliant covers of *Fortune* magazine, art-directed by Leo Lionni. My art teacher in Germany had often referred to graphic design and all its related expressions as "our cause." It was a profession that required discipline and demanded responsibility toward our audience, those who viewed the images we created, such as book and magazine covers, illustrations, typography, calligraphy, posters, and so on. I felt that the designer of *Fortune* covers must be a comrade-in-arms. So I simply phoned Leo Lionni and told him that I liked his work, I thought maybe he would like mine, and I was looking for a job.

"Come tomorrow morning at eleven o'clock," a sonorous voice told me.

Leo Lionni leafed through my portfolio and we chatted a bit. Then he looked at his wristwatch—it was noon and he invited me for lunch at his favorite restaurant, Del Pezzo, where the waiters treated us like royalty.

Back at the office, Lionni made a phone call, then scribbled on a piece of paper and handed it to me. It said, "George Krikorian, Art Director, Promotion Dept., The New York Times." Two days later, I started my job as a graphic designer at the *New York Times*.

This next scene occurred quite a few years later. Lionni was by that time an established author-illustrator of picture books and I was an art director for an advertising agency. He tried to interest me in becoming an illustrator of children's books. At that time, though, I was not very much interested, but he sent me to his editor anyway, not only once but twice. However, nothing came of it. Long before I myself was aware of it, Leo Lionni saw the picture-book artist in me.

In the busy years that followed, our paths crossed less. There was a postcard here, a phone call there, and, several years before his death in 1999, a final lunch together in Bologna with my comrade-in-arms and revered fellow artist, Leo Lionni, a true gentleman, and a most generous mentor.

—Eric Carle
October 2002

Frederick

All along the meadow where the cows grazed and the horses ran, there was an old stone wall.

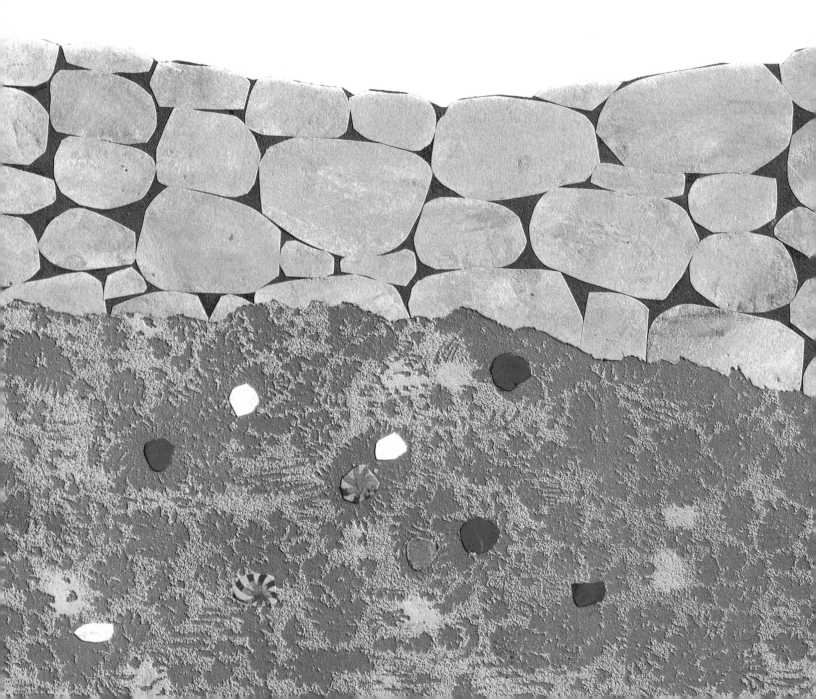

In that wall, not far from the barn and the granary,
a chatty family of field mice had their home.

But the farmers had moved away, the barn was abandoned, and the granary stood empty. And since winter was not far off, the little mice began to gather corn and nuts and wheat and straw. They all worked day and night.
All — except Frederick.

"Frederick, why don't you work?" they asked.
"I *do* work," said Frederick.
"I gather sun rays for the cold dark winter days."

And when they saw Frederick sitting there, staring at the meadow, they said, "And now, Frederick?" "I gather colors," answered Frederick simply. "For winter is gray."

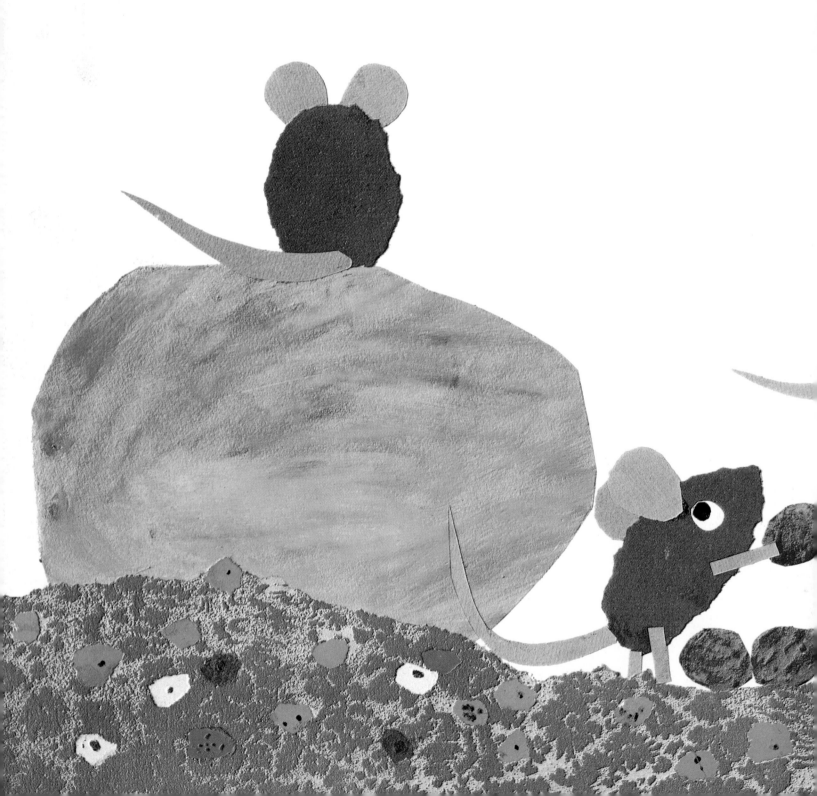

And once Frederick seemed half asleep. "Are you dreaming, Frederick?" they asked reproachfully. But Frederick said, "Oh no, I am gathering words. For the winter days are long and many, and we'll run out of things to say."

The winter days came, and when the first snow fell
the five little field mice took to their hideout in the stones.

In the beginning there was lots to eat,
and the mice told stories of foolish foxes
and silly cats. They were a happy family.

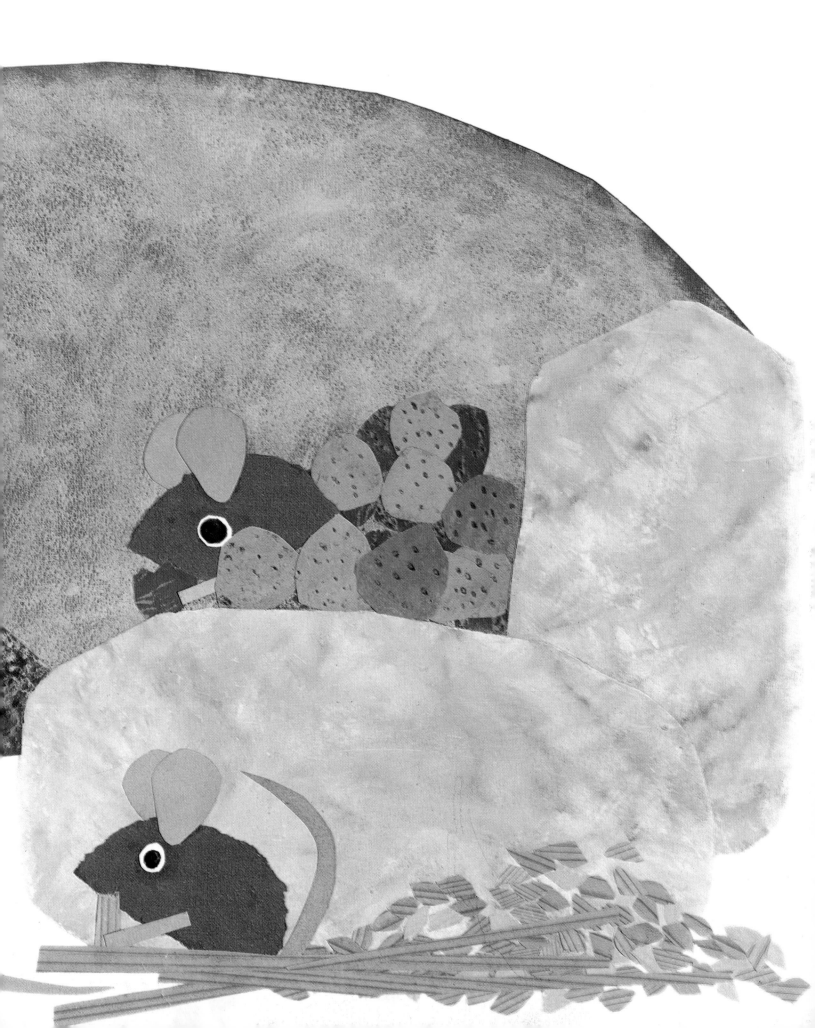

But little by little they had nibbled up
most of the nuts and berries, the straw was
gone, and the corn was only a memory.
It was cold in the wall
and no one felt like chatting.

Then they remembered
what Frederick had said about sun rays
and colors and words.
"What about *your* supplies, Frederick?"
they asked.

"Close your eyes," said Frederick,
as he climbed on a big stone.
"Now I send you the rays of the sun.
Do you feel how their golden glow..."
And as Frederick spoke of the sun
the four little mice
began to feel warmer.
Was it Frederick's voice?
Was it magic?

"And how about the colors, Frederick?"
they asked anxiously. "Close your eyes again,"
Frederick said. And when he told them
of the blue periwinkles,
the red poppies in the yellow wheat,
and the green leaves
of the berry bush,
they saw the colors as clearly
as if they had been painted
in their minds.

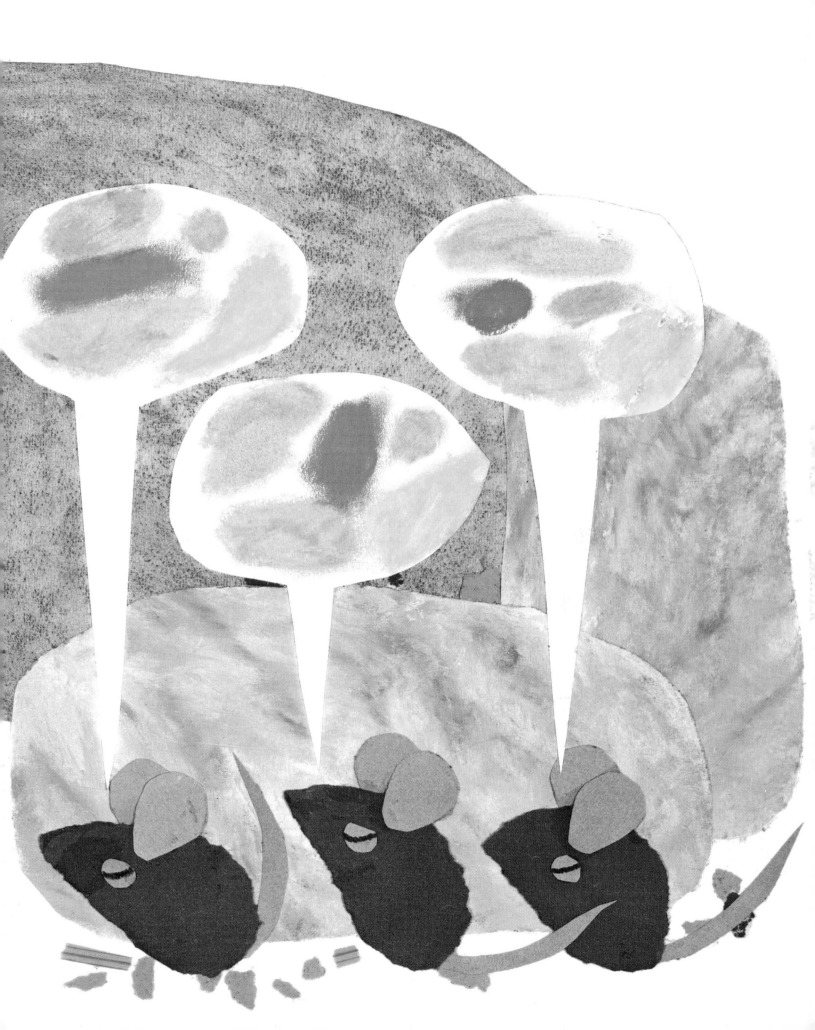

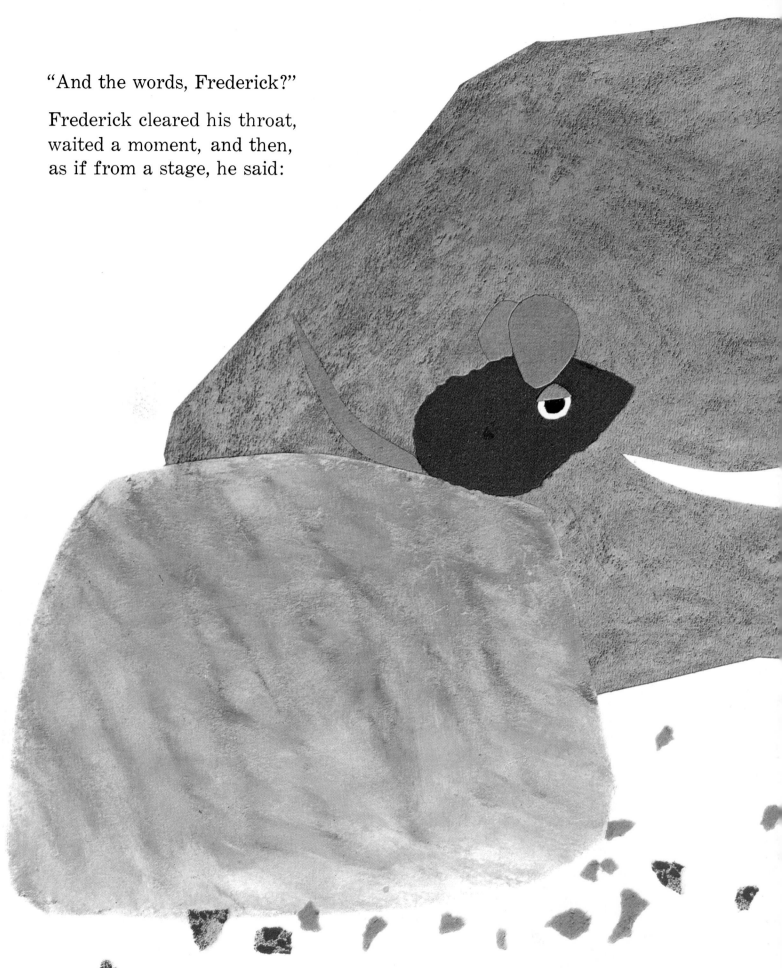

"And the words, Frederick?"

Frederick cleared his throat,
waited a moment, and then,
as if from a stage, he said:

When Frederick had finished,

"Who scatters snowflakes? Who melts the ice?
Who spoils the weather? Who makes it nice?
Who grows the four-leaf clovers in June?
Who dims the daylight? Who lights the moon?

Four little field mice who live in the sky.
Four little field mice . . . like you and I.

One is the Springmouse who turns on the showers.
Then comes the Summer who paints in the flowers.
The Fallmouse is next with walnuts and wheat.
And Winter is last . . . with little cold feet.

Aren't we lucky the seasons are four?
Think of a year with one less . . . or one more!"

they all applauded. "But Frederick," they said, "you are a poet!"

Frederick blushed, took a bow, and said shyly, "I know it."

For my friend Alfredo Segre who gave Swimmy his name.

Swimmy

A happy school of little fish lived in a corner of the sea somewhere.
They were all red. Only one of them was as black as a mussel shell.
He swam faster than his brothers and sisters. His name was Swimmy.

One bad day a tuna fish, swift, fierce and very hungry, came darting through the waves. In one gulp he swallowed all the little red fish. Only Swimmy escaped.

He swam away in the deep wet world. He was scared, lonely and very sad.

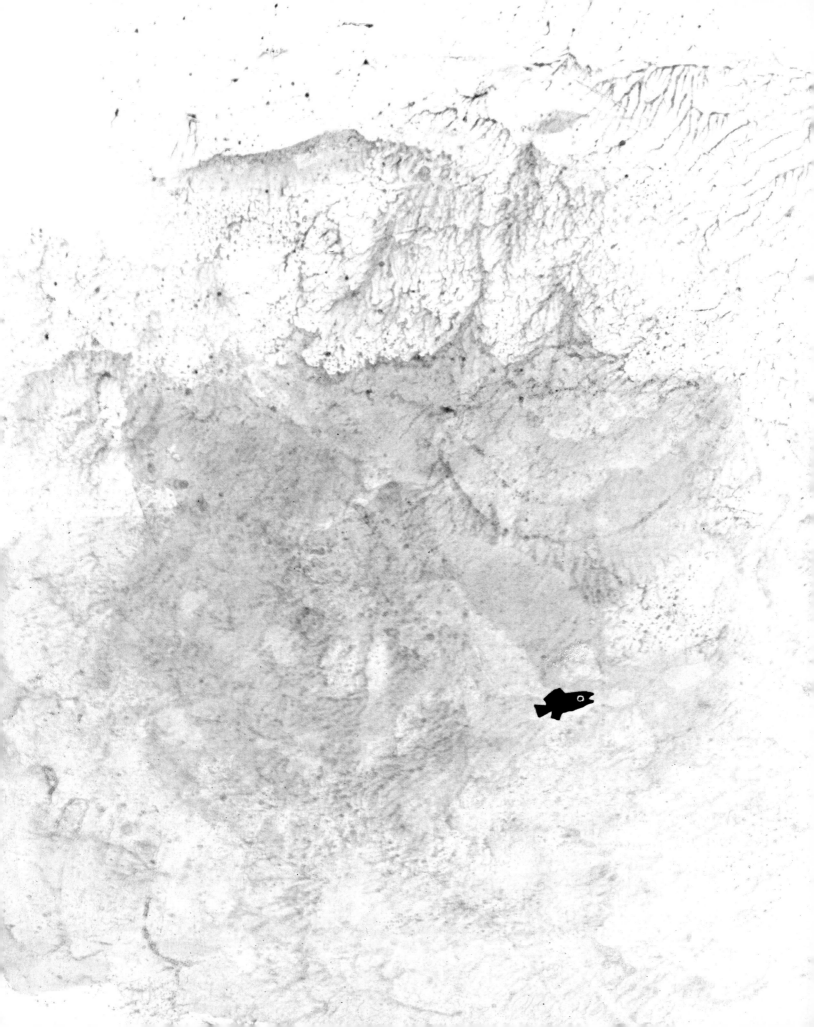

But the sea was full of wonderful creatures, and as he swam from marvel to marvel Swimmy was happy again.

He saw a medusa made of rainbow jelly…

a lobster, who walked about like a water-moving machine…

strange fish, pulled by an invisible thread...

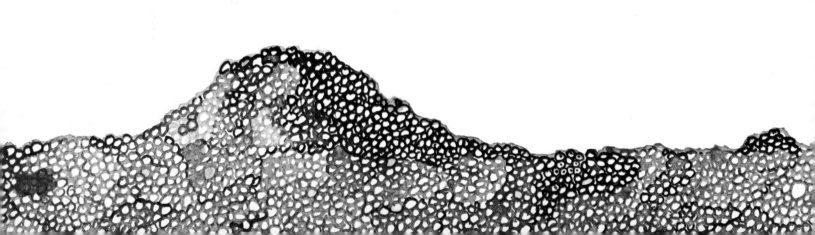

a forest of seaweeds growing from sugar-candy rocks...

an eel whose tail was almost too far away to remember…

and sea anemones, who looked like pink palm trees swaying in the wind.

Then, hidden in the dark shade of rocks and weeds, he saw a school of little fish, just like his own.

"Let's go and swim and play and SEE things!" he said happily.
"We can't," said the little red fish. "The big fish will eat us all."

"But you can't just lie there," said Swimmy. "We must THINK of something."

Swimmy thought and thought and thought.

Then suddenly he said, "I have it!"
"We are going to swim all together like the biggest fish in the sea!"

He taught them to swim close together, each in his own place,

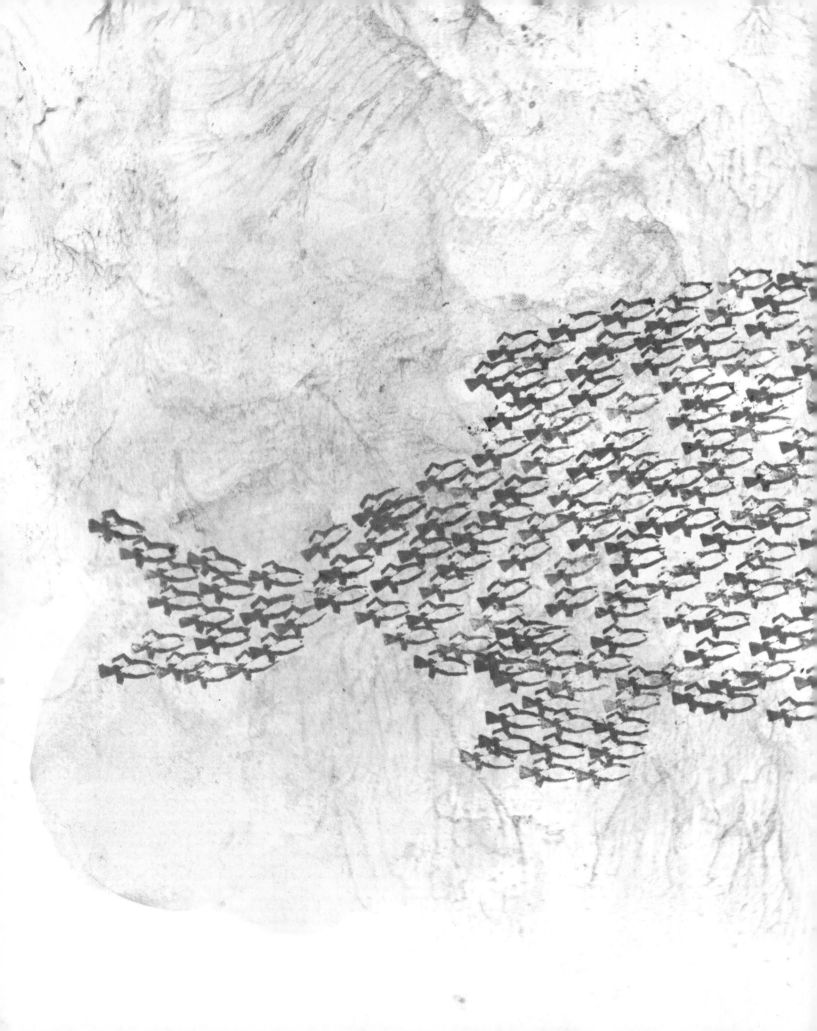

and when they had learned to swim like one giant fish, he said, "I'll be the eye."

And so they swam in the cool morning water and in the midday sun and

chased the big fish away.

Fish
is
Fish

At the edge of the woods there was a pond, and there a minnow and a tadpole swam among the weeds. They were inseparable friends.

One morning the tadpole discovered that during the night he had grown two little legs.

"Look" he said triumphantly. "Look, I am a frog!"

"Nonsense," said the minnow. "How could you be a frog if only last night you were a little fish, just like me!"

They argued and argued until finally the tadpole said, "Frogs are frogs and fish is fish and that's that!"

In the weeks that followed, the tadpole grew tiny front legs and
his tail got smaller and smaller.

And then one fine day, a real frog now, he climbed out of the water and onto the grassy bank.

The minnow too had grown and had become a full-fledged fish.
He often wondered where his four-footed friend had gone. But
days and weeks went by and the frog did not return.

Then one day, with a happy splash that shook the weeds, the frog jumped into the pond.

"Where have you been?" asked the fish excitedly.

"I have been about the world—hopping here and there," said the frog, "and I have seen extraordinary things."

"Like what?" asked the fish.

"Birds," said the frog mysteriously. "Birds!" And he told the fish about the birds, who had wings, and two legs, and many, many colors.

As the frog talked, his friend saw the birds fly through his mind like large feathered fish.

"What else?" asked the fish impatiently.

"Cows," said the frog. "Cows! They have four legs, horns, eat grass, and carry pink bags of milk."

"And people!" said the frog. "Men, women, children!" And he talked and talked until it was dark in the pond.

But the picture in the fish's mind was full of lights and colors and marvelous things and he couldn't sleep. Ah, if he could only jump about like his friend and see that wonderful world.

And so the days went by. The frog had gone and the fish just lay there dreaming about birds in flight, grazing cows, and those strange animals, all dressed up, that his friend called people.

One day he finally decided that come what may, he too must see them. And so with a mighty whack of the tail he jumped clear out of the water onto the bank.

He landed in the dry, warm grass and there he lay gasping for air, unable to breathe or to move. "Help," he groaned feebly.

Luckily the frog, who had been hunting butterflies nearby, saw him and with all his strength pushed him back into the pond.

Still stunned, the fish floated about for an instant. Then he breathed deeply, letting the clean cool water run through his gills. Now he felt weightless again and with an ever-so-slight motion of the tail he could move to and fro, up and down, as before.

The sunrays reached down within the weeds and gently shifted patches of luminous color. This world was surely the most beautiful of all worlds. He smiled at his friend the frog, who sat watching him from a lily leaf. "You were right," he said. "Fish is fish."

Alexander and the Wind-Up Mouse

"Help! Help! A mouse!" There was a scream. Then a crash.
Cups, saucers, and spoons were flying in all directions.

Alexander ran for his hole as fast as his little legs would carry him.

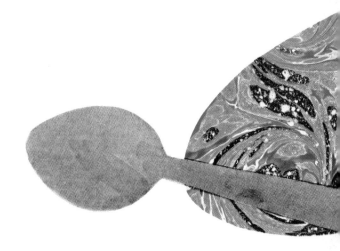

All Alexander wanted was a few crumbs and yet every time they saw him they would scream for help or chase him with a broom.

One day, when there was no one in the house, Alexander heard a squeak in Annie's room. He sneaked in and what did he see? Another mouse.
But not an ordinary mouse like himself. Instead of legs it had two little wheels, and on its back there was a key.

"Who are you?" asked Alexander.

"I am Willy the wind-up mouse, Annie's favorite toy. They wind me to make me run around in circles, they cuddle me, and at night I sleep on a soft white pillow between the doll and a woolly teddy bear. Everyone loves me."

"They don't care much for me," said Alexander sadly. But he was happy to have found a friend. "Let's go to the kitchen and look for crumbs," he said.

"Oh, I can't," said Willy. "I can only move when they wind me. But I don't mind. Everybody loves me."

Alexander, too, came to love Willy. He went to visit him whenever he could.
He told him of his adventures with brooms, flying saucers, and mousetraps.
Willy talked about the penguin, the woolly bear, and mostly about Annie.
The two friends spent many happy hours together.

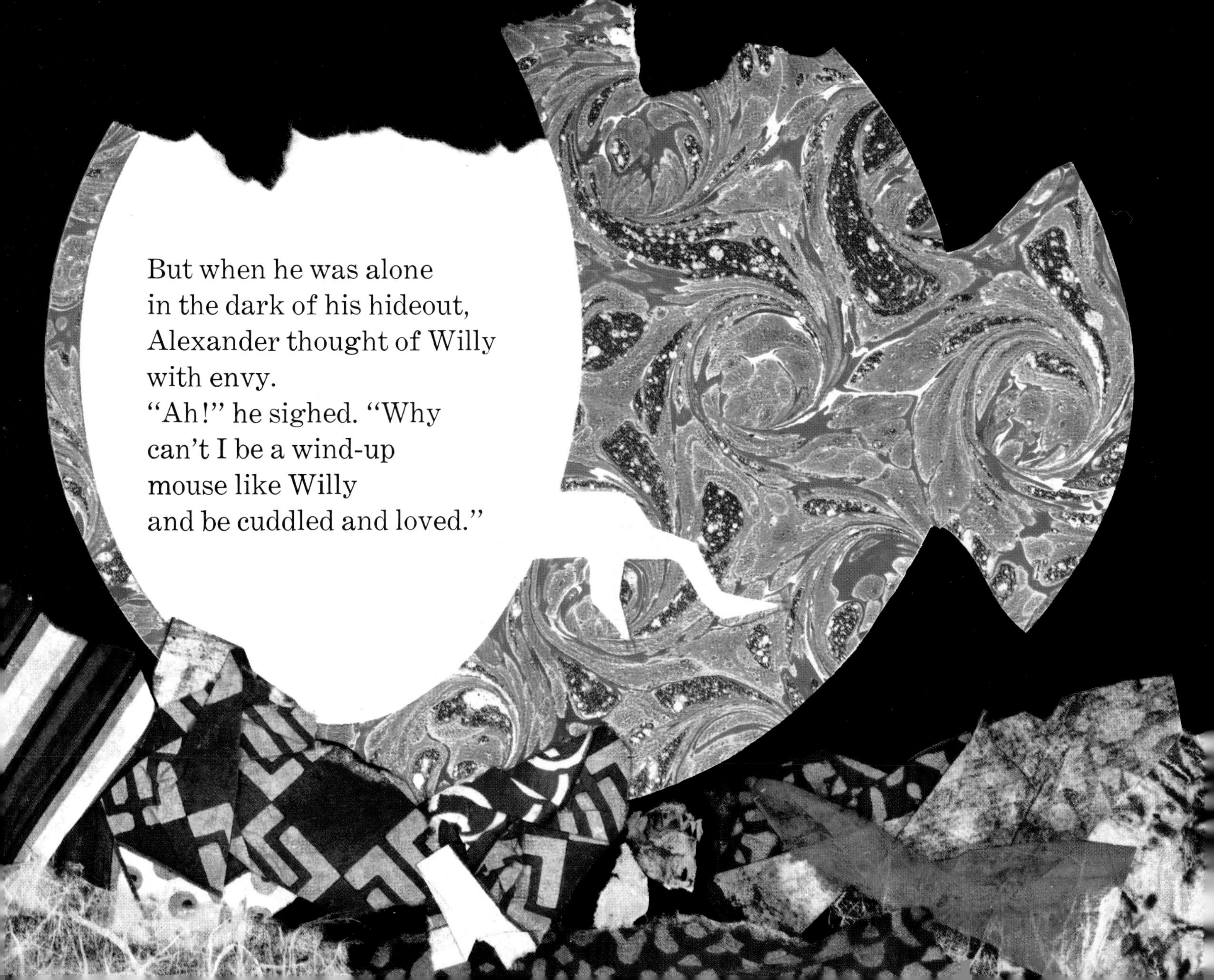

But when he was alone
in the dark of his hideout,
Alexander thought of Willy
with envy.
"Ah!" he sighed. "Why
can't I be a wind-up
mouse like Willy
and be cuddled and loved."

One day Willy told a strange story. "I've heard," he whispered mysteriously, "that in the garden, at the end of the pebblepath, close to the blackberry bush, there lives a magic lizard who can change one animal into another."

"Do you mean," said Alexander, "that he could change me into a wind-up mouse like you?"

That very afternoon Alexander went into the garden and ran to the end of the path. "Lizard, lizard," he whispered. And suddenly there stood before him, full of the colors of flowers and butterflies, a large lizard. "Is it true that you could change me into a wind-up mouse?" asked Alexander in a quivering voice.

"When the moon is round," said the lizard, "bring me a purple pebble."

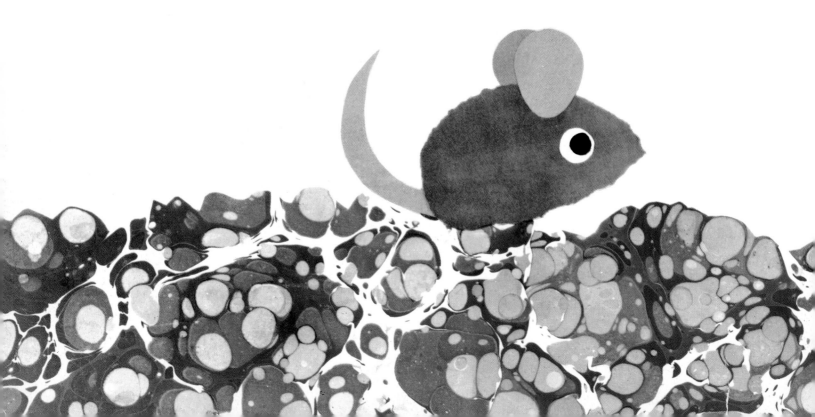

For days and days Alexander searched the garden for a purple pebble. In vain. He found yellow pebbles and blue pebbles and green pebbles—but not one tiny purple pebble.

At last, tired and hungry, he returned to the house. In a corner of the pantry he saw a box full of old toys, and there, between blocks and broken dolls, was Willy. "What happened?" said Alexander, surprised.

Willy told him a sad story. It had been Annie's birthday. There had been a party and everyone had brought a gift. "The next day," Willy sighed, "many of the old toys were dumped in this box. We will all be thrown away."

Alexander was almost in tears. "Poor, poor Willy!" he thought. But then suddenly something caught his eye. Could it really be . . . ? Yes it was! It was a little purple pebble.

All excited, he ran to the garden, the precious pebble tight in his arms. There was a full moon. Out of breath, Alexander stopped near the blackberry bush. "Lizard, lizard, in the bush," he called quickly. The leaves rustled and there stood the lizard. "The moon is round, the pebble found," said the lizard. "Who or what do you wish to be?"

"I want to be . . ." Alexander stopped. Then suddenly he said, "Lizard, lizard, could you change Willy into a mouse like me?" The lizard blinked. There was a blinding light. And then all was quiet. The purple pebble was gone.

Alexander ran back to the
house as fast as he could.

The box was there, but alas it was empty. "Too late," he thought, and with a heavy heart he went to his hole in the baseboard.

Something squeaked! Cautiously Alexander moved closer to the hole. There was a mouse inside. "Who are you?" said Alexander, a little frightened.

"My name is Willy," said the mouse.

"Willy!" cried Alexander. "The lizard . . . the lizard did it!"
He hugged Willy and then they ran to the garden path.
And there they danced until dawn.